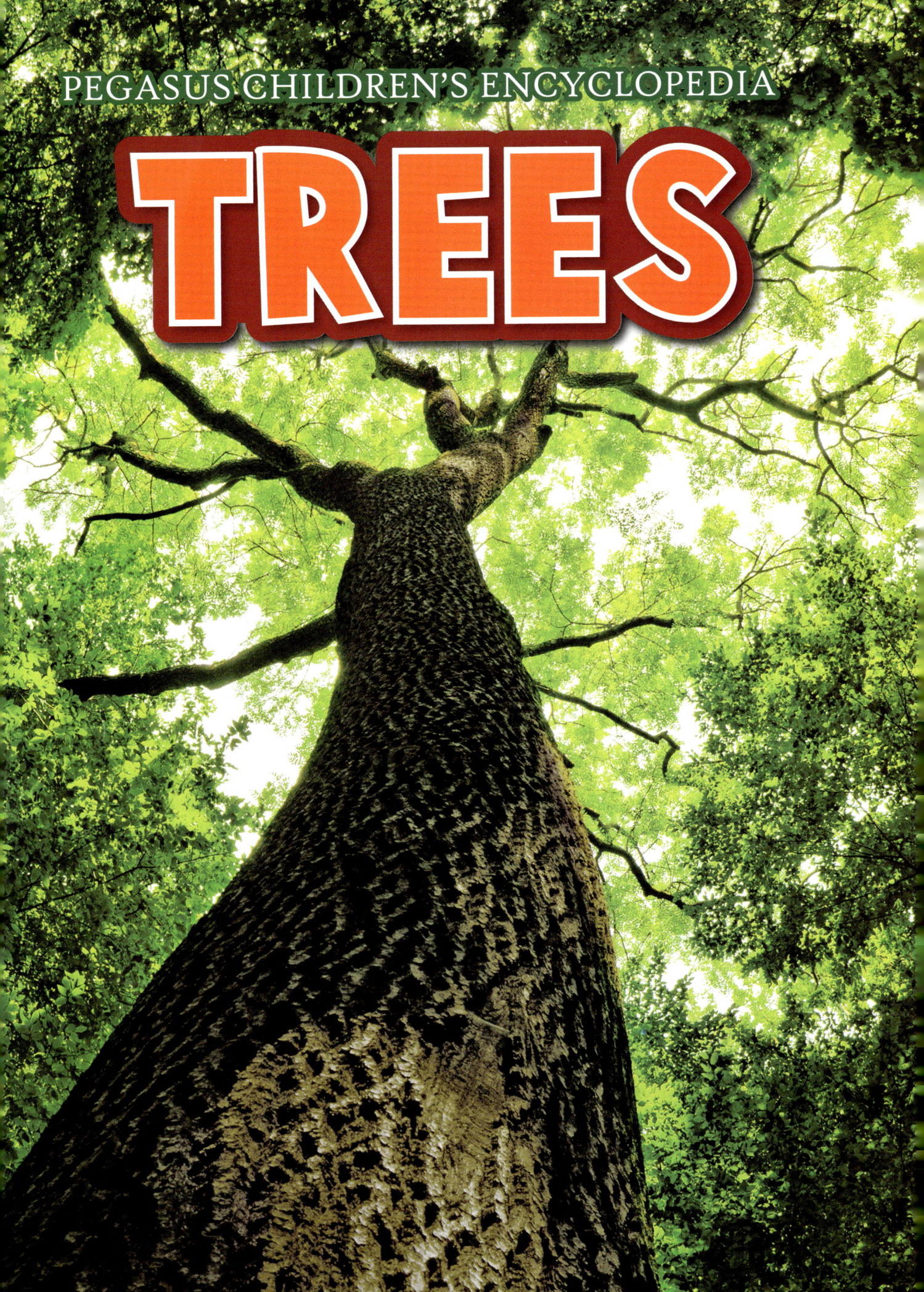

CONTENTS

What is a tree? 3

Types of trees 5

Parts of a tree 7

Reproduction and growth 10

Changing with the seasons 12

Uses of trees 14

Destruction of trees 17

Conservation of trees 19

The cultural significance of trees 21

Remarkable trees 23

Some well-known trees 25

Test Your Memory 31

Index 32

What is a tree?

Tree is a large, woody plant usually comprising of one main leafless stem (called a trunk) and several leaf-bearing stems, or branches. Each species of tree can be identified by its flowers and fruits, by the shape of its leaves, by the texture of its bark and by the structure of its branches.

Trees surpass all other plants in size and can have extremely long life spans. A few kinds of trees, such as the redwood, grow more than 100 m tall. Bristlecone pines can live more than 4,500 years. Trees thrive in temperate and moist tropical climates but cannot grow in extremely cold or dry regions.

Astonishing fact

It is estimated that there are nearly 100,000 different species of trees. The greatest diversity of tree species is found in tropical forests.

TREES

The study of trees is called **dendrology**. Trees are among the Earth's most useful and beautiful products of nature. They have been crucial to mankind's survival. The oxygen we breathe is released by trees and other plants; trees prevent erosion; trees provide food, shelter, and material for animals and man.

Trees are an important part of our daily lives. Often called nature's air conditioners, trees provide shade and relief from the sun's heat and harmful rays. They also absorb carbon dioxide and in turn, replenish the atmosphere with oxygen for us to breathe. In addition, trees make our environment more beautiful with their different colours, flowers and shapes. They give us a sense of peace and invite us to relax. Overall, trees give us a lot and ask for very little in return.

Astonishing fact

Some trees grow so slowly that it takes them 200 years to reach maturity.

Types of trees

On the basis of seeds

Gymnosperms: These are seed-bearing plants, whose seeds do not form inside the fruits, but form on the outside of the plant surface. They do not form flowers or fruits. Majority of seed-bearing plant types are gymnosperms including Conifers, Cycads, Ginkgo and Gnetales. There are between 700 and 900 species of gymnosperms in the world. Though Conifers are available in abundant numbers even now, Cycads, Ginkgo and Gnetales are all but extinct and very few species are left.

Angiosperms: These are the most dominant division of seed-bearing plants

Angiosperms

in the world today. Their distinguishing characteristics include flowers, endosperm within the seeds and the production of fruits that contain the seeds. Most of the plants that we see today are angiosperms.

Gymnosperms

Astonishing fact

Trees receive 90 per cent of their nutrition from the atmosphere and only 10 per cent from the soil!

TREES

On the basis of shedding leaves
Evergreen trees

These trees remain green all the year round; that is the trees never shed their leaves completely and have leaves throughout the seasons. Most trees belonging to the tropical rainforest and temperate warm climate are evergreens, replacing their leaves gradually throughout the year, as the leaves age and fall. Such trees more easily fall prey to pollution as compared to the deciduous varieties.

Astonishing fact

29.6 per cent of the world's land area is covered by forest. About 10 per cent of that is in Canada.

Deciduous trees

The term deciduous means 'falling off after maturity'. Such plants shed their leaves periodically, mostly during winter seasons. The process by which deciduous trees lose their leaves for a part of the year is called **abscission**. They are predominant in temperate areas with cooler climates, where winters are extreme. In areas including tropical, subtropical and arid regions of the world, the trees shed their leaves in dry summers or times with varying rainfall.

Parts of a tree

Trees have many different parts, including roots, leaves, trunk, branches and twigs, bark, cones and flowers.

Leaves and needles

The leaves of trees maybe either deciduous, meaning they come off the tree each year or evergreen staying on year round. Trees are often identified by their leaves which can be arranged on the branches in different patterns. Leaves and needles (leaves in needle like form) are the food factories on the tree's crown. Food-making or photosynthesis, begins when the sun's warmth and light is trapped by green chlorophyll in the leaves. This energy is used to combine carbon dioxide from the atmosphere with water drawn from the roots to create sugar and starch. The inner bark then carries this food to all the parts of the tree. In turn, oxygen and water are released into the atmosphere as by-products of photosynthesis.

Astonishing fact

Trees grow from the top, not from the bottom as is commonly believed. A branch's location on a tree will move up the trunk a few inches only in 1000 years!

Branches and twigs

Branches and twigs

Branches connect the trunk to the leaves and transport water and minerals to the leaves. The leaves, which are held up by branches, are arranged in a way that captures maximum sunlight. The tips of the branches are known as twigs and these are the growing ends of the tree. Leaves grow on the twigs and produce food for the whole tree, but can only do this in sunlight.

Leaves and needles

Bark

Trees have bark that is composed of layers of dead plant cells on the outside and a substance called phloem on the interior. Phloem has living cells and it helps in the transportation of food throughout the tree.

The bark of a tree has many functions. It keeps the tree from losing large amounts of water, protects the tree from insects and disease and acts as a guard against temperature extremes. The bark of a tree will change in appearance as the tree ages. Many species of trees have very distinctive bark that helps to identify them.

Bark

Trunk

Trunk

The trunk is the main stem of the tree. It supports the crown of branches, leaves/needles and transports food and water throughout the tree. The tough, outer bark protects the tree from heat, cold, moisture loss and injury. The soft inner bark carries food from the leaves and needles to all living parts of the tree. Beneath the inner bark is a thin layer called the **cambium** that each year develops new cells of inner bark on its outer wall and new sapwood cells on its inner wall. The sapwood carries water from the roots up to the leaves/needles. As the tree grows, old inner layers of sapwood die and become heartwood, a rigid fibre that gives the tree its strength.

Astonishing fact

A wild Fig Tree in South Africa holds the world record for the deepest roots as it is 121 m into the ground!

Parts of a tree

Roots

The roots act as an anchor, holding the tree firmly in place. They grow and spread out underground from the root tips, forming a huge network that draws nutrients to the tree and protects the soil from erosion. Small root hairs grow out from the roots to absorb water and minerals from the soil.

Roots

Astonishing fact

A birch tree, when fully mature can produce about a million seeds in a year!

Flowers

Cones and flowers

Trees produce flowers or cones that hold fertilized seeds. In late summer or fall, the seeds come loose and are scattered by wind, water and wildlife. Within each seed is the soft tissue that is the basis a new tree. Seeds have a tough coating that protects them during dispersal to their new home.

Cones

Reproduction and growth

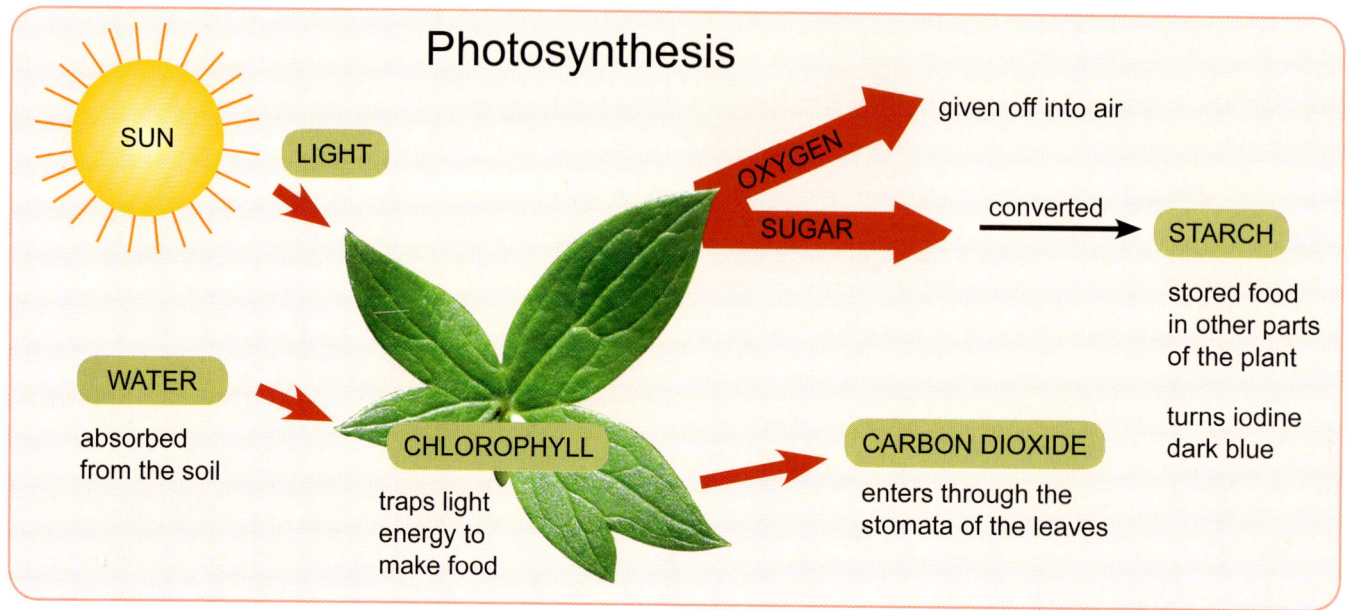

All trees (except tree ferns) have flowers by which they reproduce, in one form or another. Trees begin from seeds that have dropped to the ground from mature trees. When conditions are favourable, the cells in the seed become active and start multiplying. The basic organs such as roots, stems and leaves take form. The roots grow downward into the soil and the stem and its leaves break out above the ground.

At the tip of the new stem (which will become the main trunk of the mature tree) is a terminal bud from which growth in height of the seedling (young tree) will take place. Other buds on the stem will give rise to branches and to flowers and leaves. At the tip of each branch is a terminal bud where growth in the length of the branch takes place. Growth in the breadth of the branches and trunk takes place by division and enlargement of the cells in the cambium (plant tissue).

The basic food materials needed by trees to make new parts during the growth periods are carbohydrates. The leaves make carbohydrates through **photosynthesis**.

Reproduction and growth

Every year when a tree grows its trunk gets fatter. This is because trees don't just grow up they grow out in the form of rings too. The newest growth of a tree is between the bark and the wood that grew the year before.

Amongst the four seasons, trees usually grow best in the spring. Some parts of the world only have two seasons, wet and dry. In those areas, trees grow best in the wet season. When a tree grows its trunk gets fatter. This is because trees don't just grow up they grow out in the form of rings too. The newest growth of a tree is between the bark and the wood that grew the year before.

Wood that grows in spring develops light-coloured rings. In summers (or dry season) trees don't grow as much. Wood that grows in the summer develops dark-coloured rings.

Astonishing fact
Tree rings provide precise information about environmental events, including volcanic eruptions.

1 light-coloured ring + 1 dark-coloured ring = 1 year.

This is called a **growth ring**. A cross-section of a trunk shows these rings clearly. One can easily calculate the age of a tree by counting these rings.

The growth rings in a tree don't all look the same. This is because climate and other things going on in the environment affect a tree's growth. The temperature, the amount of rain, the quality of the soil, wind, sunlight, amount of snow on the ground and insects, all affect how a tree grows. These things are different from year to year.

Changing with the seasons

Trees undergo many changes over the course of the year. These changes are adaptations to meet the tree's needs and in response to the harshness of the climate.

During the winter, the temperature drops and the sun rides low on the horizon. Both the ground and water lie frozen. The broadleaf trees stand bare. The trees don't grow or reproduce. They are dormant.

Spring

> ### Astonishing fact
> A tree from Malaysia, Albizzia Falcata is the world's fastest growing tree. It grows so fast that it grows more than 2 cm every day!

In spring, the temperature increases, melting off the snow. There's plenty of water in the ground and the sun shines brightly. It's a time of bounty and trees develop, grow, and produce flowers and leaves.

Winter

Changing with the seasons

Picea, a species related to the fir, contains a substance used in making candy, chewing gum and medications.

Summer

Summer brings hot, sunny weather, but it's often a time of drought. Trees take this time to store reserves using photosynthesis to stabilize the new tissue that has developed.

When autumn comes around, fruit ripens and trees start preparing for the arrival of winter. Days grow shorter and the sun loses some of its strength. Leaves can no longer carry out photosynthesis and start to display their fall colours. When winter arrives, trees become dormant and the cycle begins again.

Autumn

TREES

Uses of trees

Trees are our breathing partners. People and animals depend on trees and plants for oxygen. As you breathe in, your body uses oxygen. As you breathe out, it gives off carbon dioxide. Trees do just the opposite. They take in carbon dioxide and then release oxygen.

Trees also help cool the Earth. They give off moisture. More moisture in the air means more rain and all living things need water. Trees cool the air by shading and through water evaporation. They act like huge pumps to cycle water up from the soil back into the air. The 200,000 leaves on a healthy 100 foot tree can take 11,000 gallons of water from the soil and breathe it into the air in a single growing season!

Trees are also very important for us as a renewable resource. They are a natural resource that can be renewed by the planting of trees—replacing the trees that are harvested for use by people.

We depend on forest products like the wood we burn for heat and the wood we use to make houses and furniture. We use trees for making paper for books and letters. Actually, there are more than 5,000 things made from trees. Trees give us bats, shoe polish and even toothpaste that comes from tree extracts.

Much of the wildlife on Earth will not exist without trees. In addition to releasing oxygen into the air for animals to breathe, trees provide homes and food for many animals.

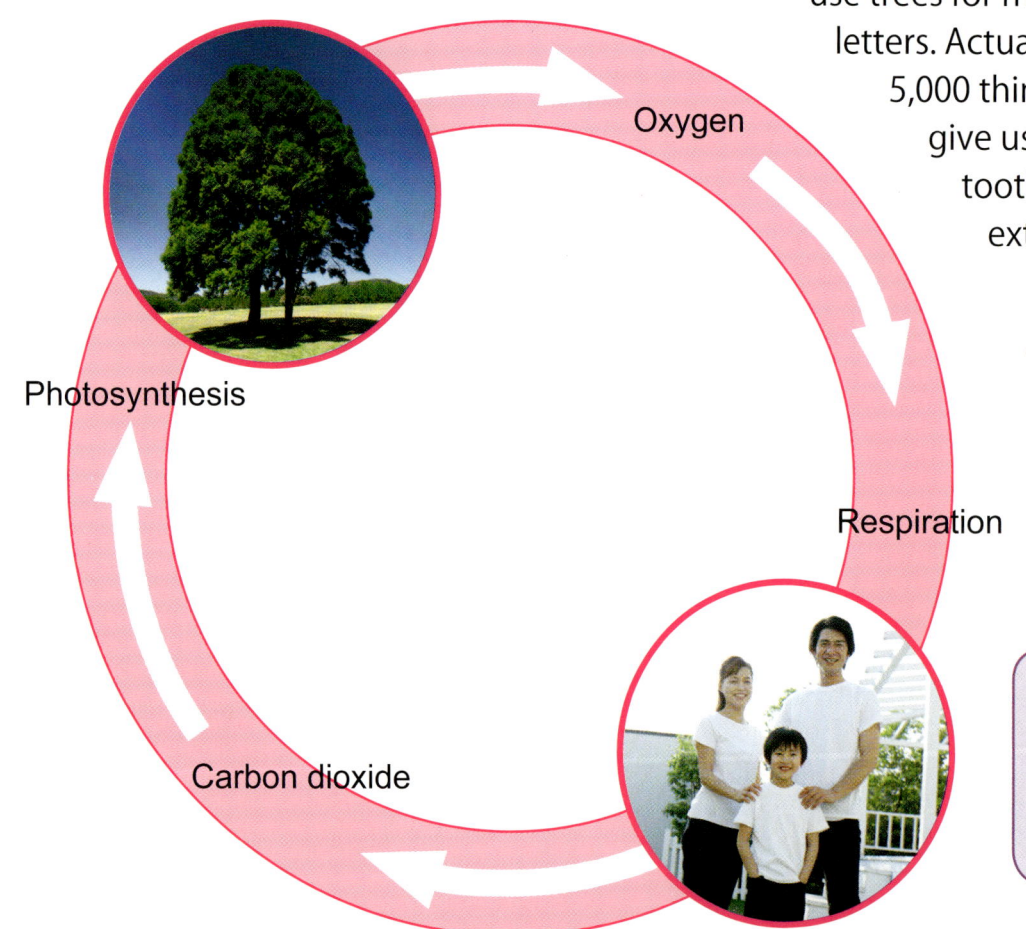

Oxygen
Photosynthesis
Respiration
Carbon dioxide

Wood from the black willow is one of the raw materials used in making polo balls.

Uses of trees

Trees have many commercial uses as well. Their wood yields thousands of products, including paper, medicines and other chemicals. Trees also provide food such as fruits, spices and nuts. Bark from the roots of the sassafras yields a tea and oils and various chemicals are derived from the roots of the longleaf pine. Some tree bark yields such substances as cork, tannins and cinnamon as well as various kinds of drugs and dyes. Some leaves, such as those of the Palmyra palm, provide fibres that are woven into twine, rope and mats. Fluids from trees yield many useful products, including rubber, maple syrup, and turpentine.

Trees are also valuable for ornamentation. They line streets and adorn gardens making them cooler and more comfortable in summer by providing shade. Among favourite shade trees is the locust, oak, elm, beech, linden, maple, birch, willow, ash, and sweet gum.

The roots of the trees hold the soil firmly and prevent soil erosion. This leads to the increase in the ground water level and the continuity of water cycle gets balanced resulting in good rains. Ultimately trees prevent drought and provide greenery to the environment. Apart from taking care of the soil and water, the trees provide shelter to many animals and birds in the forests which ultimately help in the ecological balance of the nature. Having more number of trees around will reduce the hazardous effects of global warming.

TREES

Trees can help slow down water runoff from storms by catching and storing rainfall in their canopies, then releasing the water to the atmosphere. Trees absorb the pollution in the air as well as on the ground that are usually made by humans. The carbon dioxide emitted from factories, cars and from animals all contribute to the increase of the Earth's surface temperature. The trees help lessen the rise of the Earth's surface temperature by absorbing the carbon dioxide. Meanwhile, pollution that is present on the ground, along with other nutrients in the soil is also absorbed through the roots of the trees. The trees transform these pollutants into substances that are less harmful. As a result, making the water on the ground less polluted when it reaches our local sources of water.

During windy and cold seasons, trees located on the windward side act as windbreaks. A windbreak can lower home heating bills up to 30 percent and have a significant effect on reducing snow drifts. A reduction in wind can also reduce the drying effect on soil and vegetation behind the windbreak can help keep precious topsoil in place.

> Dendrochronology is the science of calculating a tree's age by its rings.

Destruction of trees

Trees are very vulnerable. They can be damaged or hurt in many ways. Many trees are cut down every day to be made into things which humans use, like paper. Forests are sometimes burned by humans in order to get a clearing.

Many a time, nature also damages or destroys trees. For example, in long droughts, forest fires can start very easily. These fires are very hard to control and burns down nearly a whole forest!

Fungus also destroys trees. When a cut appears on a tree, fungus seeds can easily get into the sapwood of a tree. The fungus then grows up and eats away the sapwood. Soon, the wood in the trees rots and the tree collapses. Volcanoes, which are also caused by nature, are another great threat to trees. These terrible naturals disaster melts away anything in its path, including trees, by burning them up. The ashes from the volcano are poisonous and can fall into a stream or a lake. A tree which uses that as a source of water can easily die. Most natural disasters, such as an earthquake, tornado, hurricane, volcano etc. are all dangerous enemies of trees.

Trees can suffer damage from a wide variety of causes. Microorganisms cause some problems, such as root rots and needle diseases. Insects can also cause injury. However, most plant problems are due to adverse weather or cultural conditions that stress the plant. These adverse conditions include freezing, drought, over-watering, and improper fertilizing. Construction activities such as change of grade, soil compaction, mechanical injury and tree thinning can also contribute to stress.

TREES

As trees are disappearing quickly, problems are occurring. The major problem is that the animals living in the forest are being quickly destroyed. When the animals' habitat is destroyed, the animals become homeless and often die, trying to adapt to the new environment. Due to the number of forests being destroyed, many animals are becoming endangered or extinct.

Another major problem is that trees have an ability to change carbon dioxide to oxygen. But, since we destroy so many trees, it is harder to breathe now than ten years before. Not only does the process of photosynthesis allow us to breathe, but it also reduces the amount of carbon dioxide released into the atmosphere which causes global warming. Soon, the polar ice caps will melt and cause the flooding of coastal cities. If humans continue the destruction of trees, they might end up killing the human race.

Trees are also affected by air pollution, which may come from far away or very near. Pollution can slow growth or even kill trees.

Astonishing fact

Trees are the longest living organisms on Earth.

18

Conservation of trees

Trees, like us, can be affected by stress. They can also suffer from thirst, malnutrition and abuse. Like us, they breathe, take in nourishment, grow and die. Trees like us are subject to attack by disease.

Fortunately, there are treatments to care for their injuries, prevent disease, counter enemies and relieve stress. There are specialists who care for trees.

Trees have means for protecting themselves against most diseases and insects such as their bark. When healthy, most trees have nothing to worry about. There are, however, a number of factors that can weaken trees, such as too much or too little water, poor soil and injury to the trunk or roots. Any of these conditions tend to make trees more susceptible to attack.

When injured, trees react by isolating the injury site by cutting off circulation

to it. This prevents the injury from contaminating the rest of the tree. The entire tree can be affected, however, if the injury is severe. The injury site will always remain a weak point for the tree.

Insect infestations can overcome even the healthiest tree because there are just too many of them for the tree to fight effectively. Steps are taken to prevent infestations. In urgent cases, insecticides are applied to reduce the damage caused by insects.

Astonishing fact

Some species of wood ring better than any other material. That's why they are used in making musical instruments.

We can conserve trees by recycling whenever possible. Nearly all paper today can be recycled. In spite of all these efforts, far too much paper still finds its way into the garbage.

We can plant new trees every year to replace the thousands of trees cut down by industry and developers. Although, it takes several years for the new trees to develop and provide the same benefits as established forests, a continual process of planting and renewal will ensure that future forests are ready to stand and take the place of the trees that are cut down now.

Today, the people and companies that manage our nation's forests recognize that trees are a valuable resource and that it is in the best interest of each of us to conserve them. The idea of sustainable forestry means trying to keep things in balance—that is, when trees are cut down to make paper and other products, new trees are planted. Forests help wildlife by providing them food and homes. Trees and forests help us by cleaning our air, soil, and water. So we can help the world by planting a tree.

Astonishing fact

Shade of trees can make buildings up to 20 degrees cooler in the summer.

The cultural significance of trees

Astonishing fact
The average tree in a city survives only for about 8 years!

From the earliest times, trees have been the focus of religious life for many peoples around the world. Tree cults, in which a single tree or a grove of trees is worshipped, have flourished at different times almost everywhere. Even today there are sacred woods in India and Japan, just as there were in pre-Christian Europe. An elaborate mythology of trees exist across a broad range of ancient cultures.

Forests play a prominent role in many folktales and legends. With its roots buried deep in the Earth, its trunk above ground and its branches stretching toward the sky, a tree serves as a symbolic, living link between this world and those of supernatural beings. In many myths, a tree is a vital part of the structure of the universe. Gods and their messengers travel from world to world by climbing up or down the tree. The Norse (the Scandinavian people before the Christianization of Scandinavia) believed that a tree runs like an axis or pole, through this world and the realms above and below it. They called their World Tree Yggdrasill. It was a great ash tree that nourished gods, humans and animals, connecting all living things and all phases of existence.

TREES

The mythology of early India, preserved in texts called the Upanishads, includes a cosmic tree called **Asvattha**. It is the living universe, an aspect of Brahma, the world spirit. This cosmic tree reverses the usual order. Its roots are in the sky and its branches grow downward to cover the earth.

Providers of shade and bearers of fruit, trees have long been associated with life and fertility. Evergreen trees, which remain green all year, became symbols of undying life. Deciduous trees, which lose their leaves in the winter and produce new ones in the spring, symbolized renewal, rebirth after death or immortality.

Another belief about trees sees them as embodying deities, spirits or simply humans changed into trees by a special fate. Some Celtic and other European peoples worshiped groves of trees as well as particular trees. In the religion of the Druids (a member of the priestly class in Gaul and possibly other parts of western Europe) oaks were sacred. The ancient Romans associated oak trees with their sky God, Jupiter. In Greek and Roman mythology, Dryads were nymphs who lived in trees and perished when their trees died or were cut down.

> Knocking on wood for good luck originated from primitive tree worship when rapping on trees was believed to summon protective spirits in the trees.

Remarkable trees

Astonishing fact
The death of one 70 year old tree would return over three tons of carbon into the atmosphere.

Sunland Baobab—world's stoutest tree

Sunland Baobab, an African Baobab located in Sunland Farm, Limpopo in South Africa is the stoutest tree in the world with a diameter of 10.64 m and a circumference of 33.4 m. This popular tourist attraction has a bar and a wine cellar inside its hollowed trunk. It is also the largest baobab in the world.

Hyperion—world's tallest living tree

This Coast Redwood tree named Hyperion in California, USA, is the record holder for the tallest known living organism in the world with a confirmed measurement of 115.61 m tall. The Hyperion is estimated to contain 502 m^3 of wood and to be roughly 700-800 years old.

Methuselah – world's oldest tree

The oldest measured tree is the Great Basin Bristlecone Pine named Methuselah. Its confirmed age is 4,845 years! Alerce Fitzroya cupressoides is 2nd oldest with a verified age of 3,267 years.

TREES

Pygmy Pine – world's smallest tree

The smallest known tree in the world is the Pygmy Pine. It is a species of conifer which is native to New Zealand. Its branches maybe up to 5 mm in diameter and up to 1 m long. It is rarely bigger than a small low-growing shrub. It is also known as Mountain Rimu.

General Sherman – world's largest tree

General Sherman is one of the tallest Giant Sequoia trees in the world with a height of about 84.8 m. Although not the tallest tree in the world, it is the biggest in terms of volume, making it the world's largest known single organism by volume. The volume of its trunk measures about 1487 cubic metres. The tree is located in the Giant Forest of Sequoia National Park in US. The tree is believed to be between 2,300 and 2,700 years old. It was named after General William Tecumseh Sherman, American Civil War leader in 1879.

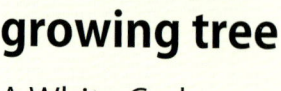

Trees lower air temperature by evaporating water in their leaves.

White Cedar— the slowest growing tree

A White Cedar located in the Great Lakes area of Canada, has grown less than 4 inches tall during its 155 years – the slowest growing tree recorded so far.

Some well-known trees

Tree of Life – Bahrain

The Tree of Life in Bahrain is a 400 year-old mesquite tree which lives in the middle of a desert. This well matured tree has come to be known as the **Tree of life** because of the mystery surrounding its existence in the middle of the desert without any known water source. The fact that is stands alone in this area has further raised the curiosity of visitors and specialist alike for many years.

The mystery of the survival of the tree has made it a legend and the name 'tree of life' is absolutely appropriate for the tree, truly representing the magic of life. A legend is also attached to the site where the tree is located. The local inhabitants believe that this was the actual location of the Garden of Eden!

Cedars of God – Lebanon

The astonishing Cedars of God are among the most spectacular trees in the world. They are the last survivors of the immense forests of the Cedars of Lebanon that thrived across Mt. Lebanon in ancient times. Their timber was used by the early civilizations like Phoenicians, Assyrians, Babylonians and Persians. The famous Biblical character King Solomon also used these Cedars in building temples during his time.

Today it is a small forest of about 400 Lebanon Cedar trees on Mount Lebanon. The trees are remnants of what used to be a thick forest in the mountains of Lebanon during biblical times. The Cedars of Lebanon are mentioned in the Bible more than 70 times. Today, the Cedars of God is listed as a UNESCO World Heritage Site and is strictly protected by the Lebanese government.

Pirangi Cashew Tree, Brazil

Upon approaching the world's largest cashew tree, you might think you are entering a forest. But despite covering about 8,500 sq m, it is indeed a single tree. The 117-year-old tree, which is 80 times larger than an average cashew tree, currently takes up an area larger than a soccer field and bears 80,000 fruits per year.

The world's largest cashew tree, also known as the Pirangi cashew, is located in Pirangi beach in Parnamirim, 12 km south to the capital city of Natal, in the state of Rio Grande do Norte (Brazil). The tree covers an area of approximately 8500 sq m, with a perimeter of approximately 500 m and produces about eighty thousand cashews per year. The cashew was planted in 1888 by a fisherman named Luiz Inácio de Oliveira. He died, aged 93 years, under the shadows of the cashew. In 1994, the cashew tree entered the Guinness Book of Records.

TREES

Baobab Tree, Madagascar

Baobabs, with their distinctive shape, are one of the most charismatic groups of trees in the world. Six out of the eight species of baobab are typical to Madagascar, three are classified as 'endangered' and three are near threatened.

Baobab trees maybe the oldest life forms on the African continent and many that are still standing today have been around since Roman times. They are leafless for most of the year, and their thick, bloated, fire-resistant trunks store water during the dry months. Some baobab trunks are so large that people live inside them. Arabian legend about the baobab says 'the devil plucked up the baobab, thrust its branches into the earth and left its roots in the air'.

The baobab tree has an enormous trunk with tapering branches and can attain a maximum height of 22.9 m and maximum diameter of 18.2 m around the trunk. It is also one of the longest lived trees in the world. Carbon dating indicates that they may live to be 3,000 years old!

Astonishing fact

A man owning a White Oak in Athens willed 5.9 sq m of land (on which the tree grew) in its name! He probably did this to show that the Oak tree owned that particular land so that no one would ever chop it down!

Sri Maha Bodhi

Jaya Sri Maha Bodhi is a Sacred Fig tree in Anuradhapura, Sri Lanka. It is said to be a sapling from the historical Bodhi tree under which Buddha became enlightened. It was planted in 288 BC, and is the oldest living human-planted tree in the world with a known planting date.

It was planted on a high terrace about 6.5 m above the ground and surrounded by railings, and today it is one of the most sacred relics of the Buddhists in Sri Lanka and respected by Buddhists all over the world. This wall was constructed during the reign of King Kirthi Sri Rajasingha, to protect it from wild elephants which might have damaged the tree.

The tree is said to be the southern branch of the Sri Maha Bodhi Tree at Bodh Gaya in India under which Buddha attained Enlightenment.

In the 3rd century BC, the Buddha's fig tree was brought to Sri Lanka by the Thera Sanghamitta, daughter of Emperor Ashoka and founder of an order of Buddhist nuns in Sri Lanka. In 249 BC, Siri Maha Bodhi was planted in the Mahameghavana Park in Anuradhapura by King Devanampiyatissa.

Major Oak of Sherwood Forest – England

Situated in the heart of Sherwood Forest, this legendary tree is more than 800 years old. It is also the largest oak tree in England. Legend has it that Robin Hood once hid in the hollow of the Major Oak.

The sheer size of the tree is remarkable. It has a height of 19 m, the girth of the main trunk is 10 m and the spread of the branches and leaves is 28 m.

The number of visitors to the tree each year is currently estimated to be 900,000, one very good reason why it is now fenced off. The Major Oak still produces good crops of acorns every three or four years. In a good year it will produce over 150,000 acorns!

Test Your MEMORY

1. What is a tree?

2. What is the study of trees called?

3. Name the types of trees.

4. Discuss about the parts of a tree.

5. How do trees reproduce?

6. How do trees change with seasons?

7. Write three uses of trees.

8. How are trees damaged?

9. How can we conserve trees? Suggest 2 ways.

10. Write about the cultural significance of trees.

11. Write two sentences about the Baobab tree.

12. What are the Cedars of God?

Index

A
abscission 6
angiosperms 5
Asvattha 22

B
bark 3, 7, 8, 11, 15, 19
branches 3, 7, 8, 10, 21, 22, 24, 28, 30
broadleaf trees 12

C
cambium 8, 10
carbohydrates 10
carbon dioxide 4, 7, 10, 14, 16, 18
cones 7, 9

D
deciduous trees 6, 22
Dendrology 4
dormant 12, 13
Druids 22
Dryads 22

E
environment 4, 11, 15, 18
evergreen trees 6, 22

F
flowers 3, 4, 5, 7, 9, 10, 12

G
global warming 15, 18
growth rings 11
gymnosperms 5

M
microorganisms 17
moisture 8, 14

O
oxygen 4, 7, 10, 14, 18

P
Phloem 8
photosynthesis 7, 10, 13, 14, 18
pollution 6, 16, 18

R
reproduce 10, 12
roots 7, 8, 9, 10, 15, 16, 19, 21, 22, 28

S
seeds 5, 9, 10, 17
soil erosion 15
stems 3, 8, 10

T
terminal bud 10
tree cults 21
trunk 3, 7, 8, 10, 11, 19, 21, 23, 24, 28, 30
twigs 7

W
water evaporation 14
water runoff 16
windbreaks 16

Y
Yggdrasill 21